To Jeff

Thank you to my family
and a special thank you to Laura Godwin

Henry Holt and Company, Inc., *Publishers since 1866*
115 West 18th Street, New York, New York 10011

Henry Holt is a registered trademark of Henry Holt and Company, Inc.

Published in Canada by Fitzhenry & Whiteside Ltd., 195 Allstate Parkway, Markham, Ontario L3R 4T8.

Library of Congress Cataloging-in-Publication Data
Coursen, Valerie.
Mordant's Wish / Valerie Coursen.
Summary: After wishing that a turtle-shaped cloud could be his friend, Mordant the mole
finds his wish spurring a series of unusual events.
[1. Wishes—Fiction. 2. Moles (Animals)—Fiction. 3. Clouds—Fiction.
4. Turtles—Fiction. 5. Friendship—Fiction.] I. Title.
PZ7.C831565Mo 1997 [E]—dc21 96-44210
ISBN 0-8050-4374-8
First Edition—1997
Typography by Martha Rago
The artist used gouache on watercolor paper to create the illustrations for this book.
Printed in the United States of America on acid-free paper. ∞
1 3 5 7 9 10 8 6 4 2

Mordant's Wish

Valerie Coursen

Henry Holt and Company

New York

Mordant the mole,
deep in his damp little hole,
stared up at the sky.
Above him was a cloud shaped like a turtle.
I wish that turtle were real, thought Mordant.
I wish that turtle were my friend.

He scurried out of his hole.
How could he make his wish come true?

Mordant blew on a dandelion puff.
I wish that turtle were real, he thought.
I wish that turtle were my friend.
He kept on blowing and wishing,
and wishing and blowing,
until the air was full of feathery white seeds.

Calum, on his bike, whizzed through the white.
Are my eyes playing tricks on me? he wondered.
This looks like snow.

Snow made him think of snow cones, so...
to *Velma's Famous Snow Cones* he rode.

Some of his snow cone
dripped
dripped
dripped
into a small puddle.

Peanut, a bird, was perched high above Velma's shop.

Peanut looked down at the puddle
and saw the shape of a hat,
the same shape as the hat
that belonged to dear Aunt Nat!

Peanut flapped his wings and flew off
to visit her.

Aunt Nat was so happy
to see Peanut
that out of her beak
came the happiest song.
Peanut chirped along.

Mr. Ricardo, a barber, heard the song and began to hum.

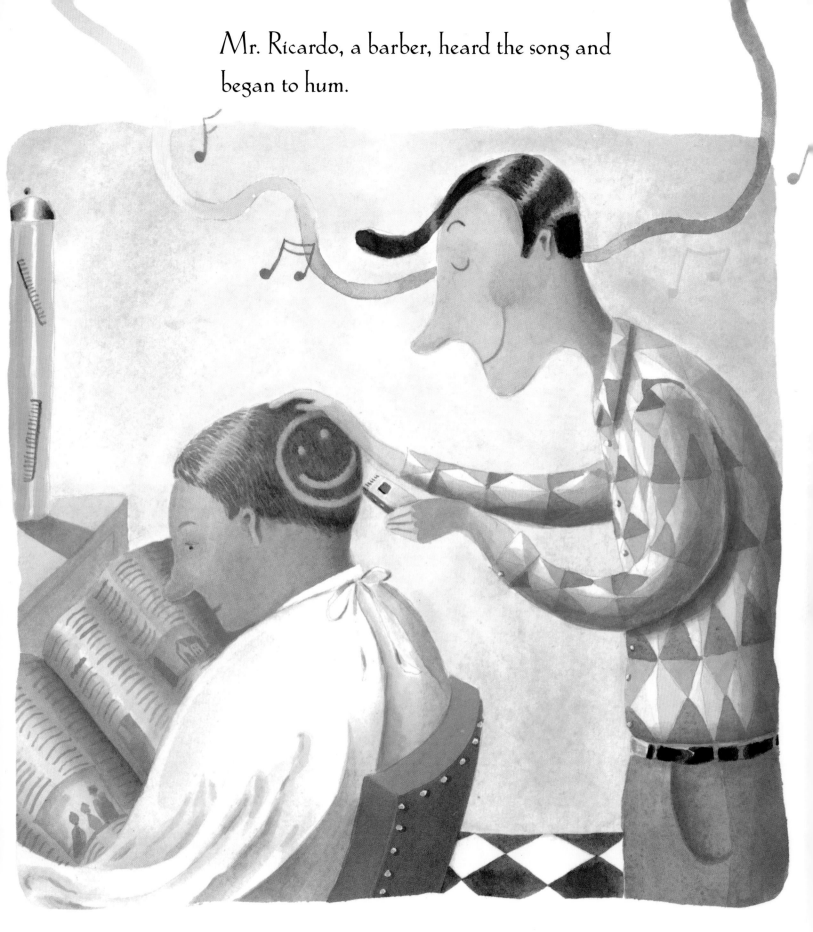

He was so happy humming he did not notice
what he was shaving on the back of Mr. Took's head.

Mr. Took walked up the street
to the Fine Fine Antiques shop.
He liked to look in the shop window.

In that window Blanche, a beetle,
lived in a button bowl.

That very moment, Blanche was crying
a thousand beetle tears into a tiny beetle hanky.

Why was Blanche so upset?
Because her favorite buttons, the pearl ones
with the red roses painted on them, had just been sold.
Yes, all of them—*sold!*

Blanche was sure nothing
could be worse.
She sobbed and stared out
the shop window
in dismay.

Then through her tears she saw an amazing sight.
Even though she had seen Mr. Took many times before,
she had never seen him with such a daring haircut.

The sight of it cheered her right up.
It made her forget all about the buttons.
It made her feel like doing something daring herself.
So before she could think about it, she hopped onto a package
that was going out the door, and then onto a flowery dress.

With the flick of a finger
Blanche went flying through the air.

And where do you think she landed?

She landed in a sweet–smelling red rose.

Blanche thought the flower
was much better than rose–painted buttons.
She nestled into the soft petals
and decided this would be her new home.

Now what?

Well, did you notice that
as she was rushing along
the woman in the flowery dress
dropped her shopping list?

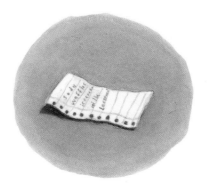

There it lay on the sidewalk.

Most everyone walked on by.

But Petunia May stopped and picked it up.
She considered it quite a find.
She liked to collect keys that people drop,
broken umbrellas that get tossed aside,
school papers that are blown away,
and flattened-out mittens or gloves.

Shopping lists were the most interesting, though.
There were hidden messages in them.

This one was clearly telling her to *SWIM*.

Petunia May rounded up her friends
and set off for the lake.

Near the lake was a busy road where cars whizzed by.
Every day a turtle sat on the edge of the road.
He longed to know who lived at the top of the hill
on the other side.

But he was afraid to cross the road.
Day after day he stretched out his neck and
watched the cars zooming past.

One afternoon the turtle felt particularly brave,
so he stepped onto the road.
Whoosh! A car roared past.
The turtle ducked back into his shell.
I'll never make it, he thought.

Just then, he heard voices and
felt himself being lifted
and carried
and gently placed on the ground again.

After a moment he poked his head
out of his shell.
Where was he?

Why, on the other side, of course.

The turtle looked up the hill.
Today I will find out who lives
at the top, he thought.

And he did.